U
in the Attic

Springy and Sam

Uncle
in the Attic

Jan Needle

Illustrated by Kate Aldous

MAMMOTH

For
Sadie Supergirl

First published in Great Britain 1987
by William Heinemann Ltd
Published 1990 by Mammoth
an imprint of Mandarin Paperbacks
Michelin House, 81 Fulham Road, London SW3 6RB

Mandarin is an imprint of the Octopus Publishing Group

Copyright © Jan Needle 1987

ISBN 0 7497 0075 0

A CIP catalogue record for this title
is available from the British Library

Printed in Great Britain
by Cox & Wyman Ltd, Reading, Berkshire

Contents

1 · Cowboys

'The trouble with your brother Arthur,' said Mum angrily, 'is he's a cowboy. I knew this would happen! I just knew it.'

Two of the removal men were passing as she said this, carrying a large wardrobe towards The Kerry. Springy and Sam thought they would be interested to hear there was a cowboy in the family, but they just grunted off along the front garden path.

Dad grinned at their mother.

'Give over, Jean,' he said. 'He's broken his wrist. You can't blame a feller for breaking his wrist.'

Mrs Jean Price snorted.

'Knowing Arthur,' she said, 'he's probably done it on purpose. The thought of all the work that's waiting for him here was too much for him. He's an idle, useless cowboy.'

'Mum,' said Springy, 'Uncle Arthur's not a cowboy. He's a painter.'

'When does he ever paint?' said his mother. She turned and started to stamp off towards the front door. She was furious. 'If he hasn't broken his wrist he's got a cold. If he hasn't got a cold he's got a bad leg. He's a lazy good-for-nothing.'

'Yes,' said Springy. 'But that doesn't make him a cowboy, does it?'

Because his Mum had disappeared into the house, Springy's father answered.

'It's just something you call a bad workman,' he said. 'It's because cowboys didn't like being bossed about. They wandered all over the prairies in the Wild West and nobody could give them orders.'

Sam said: 'They could have telephoned.'

Springy and his father looked at her to see if she was joking, but they couldn't tell. She was all grin and freckles, was Sam, with lots of bright ginger hair. She was always playing jokes on them.

Springy began to tell her, seriously, that they didn't have telephones in the Wild West, but his mother stomped out of the house again.

'Don't just stand there, Jeff,' she snapped. 'Get those kids helping. Up to the attic, Sam, and down to the cellar, Springy. Unpack the cardboard boxes marked URGENT.'

'Oh Mum,' moaned Sam. 'Why do *I* have to climb all the stairs?'

'Because your brother's too lazy,' said Mum.

'By the time he got to the attic he'd be asleep. Now – shift.'

Springy and Sam – who were twins, but completely different – dragged slowly into the house and stood about in the hallway. They wanted to explore, not work.

'It's not fair,' said Sam. 'We've never had a new house to look at. It's enormous. I want to crawl about before it all gets tidied up.'

Springy laughed.

'That'll be ages,' he replied. 'If Uncle Arthur's broken his wrist, how's the decorating going to get done? Who's going to do the painting? Dad's only got the weekend off.'

'Heck,' said Sam. 'I hadn't thought of that. Mum'll go hairless. She said if she can't let some rooms soon, we won't be able to pay the mortgage.'

'Whatever that is,' agreed Springy. 'Fancy buying a house you can't afford. They're potty, our Mum and Dad.'

'Mind your backs, kids,' said the biggest of the removal men. He was carrying a kitchen cabinet all by himself. 'It's a great big house you've got here. Are you going to keep an elephant in the back garden?'

The twins pressed themselves against the passage wall so that he could get by. Then they heard their mother coming back to the front door. They scuttled towards the kitchen, turned left, zipped down the cellar stairs, and ran through three cellars to the bottom door into the garden. They didn't feel like work.

The garden was brilliant. It wasn't big, but it was like a jungle, with a huge tangle of bushes in one corner, a tumbledown shed, waist-high weeds everywhere, and not a flower in sight.

'You could, couldn't you?' said Sam. 'I wonder how much it would cost to feed?'

Springy knew what she was talking about without having to ask. That happened a lot to

them. Because they were twins, said Auntie Violet, who could read the future.

'Never mind feeding it,' he said. 'Where would we get one? Elephants don't grow on trees. They're too heavy.'

'Look,' said Sam, who was poking about behind the old shed. 'Rabbit hutches! So people *have* kept pets here.'

It must have been a long time ago, however. The hutches were even wonkier than the shed. The doors were hanging off, and the wire was torn and rusted into holes big enough to put a donkey through.

'You couldn't use them now,' said Springy. 'Anyway, I don't want a rabbit. I want a dog.'

His sister laughed.

'You'll be lucky,' she said. 'Mum says you're too lazy for a dog. She says you don't even exercise *yourself* unless you're forced to!'

She paused.

'*I* could have a dog,' she went on, smugly. 'But I think dogs are boring.'

Normally, they could have argued for ages about this, because they both wanted a pet very badly, and they had never been able to have one. The place they had last lived in had been a flat, with only a window box that wasn't even big enough to graze a caterpillar on. But today, there was too much excitement in the air to have a row.

'Look,' said Springy. 'Why's that back fence so high? What's that funny noise?'

They listened for a moment or two, then started pushing through the bushes and weeds towards the end of the garden. The noise was a hollow ponking sound, that they half recognised.

When they pulled and pushed the branches and leaves away they knew where they'd heard it. On the television, in the summer. It was the noise of tennis balls hitting rackets. Behind the high wire fence was a little tennis club, just three courts, with some people dressed in white, knocking balls to each other over nets. Springy and Sam were delighted.

'Hey,' said Sam. 'We can join! We can learn to play! We can get to be tennis stars!'

Springy watched for a moment or two. The people were running about in the sunshine, and sweating.

'It looks like dead hard work,' he said. 'I think I'll stick to model planes.'

As if by magic, at the sound of the word 'work', their mother shouted for them. She did not sound happy.

'Springy!' she yelled. 'Samantha! Come in here at once. Something terrible's happened.'

'Samantha!' said Sam. 'It *must* be terrible.'

'It can't be the end of the world, though,' said Springy. 'At least she didn't call me Stephen.'

'Stephen!' screeched his mother. 'If you're not on this doorstep in two seconds I'll skin the pair of you. I need you *now*!'

'Crikey Moses,' said Springy. 'First of all it was cowboys. Now it sounds as if the Indians have come! Heap big mother on the warpath!'

Mum had got fed up with waiting. They could hear her crashing through the bushes towards them like an escaped rhino.

'I'm going thataway,' said Sam, pointing. 'Race you to the door.'

She ran along a path, and her brother crept through the long grass. When Mum finally came back from searching the garden, they were on the step, waiting for her.

'Where have *you* been?' asked Sam, innocently.

But Mum was in no mood for jokes.

'One word of cheek,' she said, 'and you're in real trouble. Both of you.'

'Oh,' said Springy. 'What's up?'

'Everything,' said Mrs Price. 'It couldn't be worse. This whole business has turned into a disaster.'

She left them to follow her through the open kitchen door.

2 · What A Way to Spend Saturday

When Springy and Sam walked into the kitchen, they knew immediately what the trouble was. Their father was leaning against the wall looking utterly fed up – and sitting near him, at the small red formica table on an upside down tea chest, was John Sugden.

As The Kerry had been a boarding house (and was to be one again), it was full of peculiar rooms. The kitchen was one of the oddest.

Any sensible boarding house, you might think, would have a large, airy well-planned kitchen, so that lots of breakfasts and teas could be cooked easily, in a hurry. The Kerry did not.

It was a small room, shaped like an 'L', with too many sinks and too many cupboards. The table was tiny, and Springy and Sam could not begin to work out where all the chairs would go.

Off it led another room, equally odd, which was where people would eat, after the food had been cooked. This was dark and miserable, without even a window. One wall was covered in brown panelling made of mock wood. The whole thing, in fact, was more like a grim prison than a cheery breakfast room.

But this – for the moment – was not Mrs Price's problem. The problem was the fat man with the blue boiler suit and the bald pink head. He was talking to their father in a very serious voice.

'It's no good saying you can't, Jeff, because you can. I know I said I'd try to give you the time off, but what am I to do?'

Mr Price made an angry movement with his hand.

'It's Friday night, John. My brother can't turn up to help because he's broken his wrist, and the wife and kids can't cope. All I need is two days to get the place straight. Two days which I asked for anyway.'

Mrs Price butted in: 'And which are Saturday and Sunday, John. The *weekend*. Remember what that means?'

John Sugden put on a sorry face.

'Jean,' he said. 'Believe me, love. There's a load to get to Aberdeen and there's no other man to take it. Weekend or no weekend, Jeff's got to do the run.'

Sam said: 'But it's not any old weekend. We're moving in.'

Springy added: 'If we don't get guests in soon, we're broke.'

Mum tutted angrily to make him shut up. Springy glared at her.

'It's you that said it, Mum,' he said. 'You said we couldn't pay the mortgage.'

She shook her head and turned to her husband.

'Jeff, get these kids working, will you? I can't. If I've told them once I've said it a dozen times. Springy, into that cellar and cool off. There's hundreds of boxes wanting emptying.'

'What about her, then?'

His father raised a finger.

'Shift! And you, Sam! Make yourselves useful, can't you!'

The twins mooched off, this time to work. Although Springy, who had been born idle, only made it as far as the lavatory at the top of the stairs. He locked the door and sat down with a comic. He did not read it, though. He was too fed up with his father.

Downstairs, through the open window, he could hear the voices rumbling on. He knew what the upshot would be, there was never any difference. Dad was a lorry driver, therefore Dad

was often away. Even on special weekends like this one, he could get sent at a moment's notice. Sometimes he wasn't seen for days on end. Sometimes for weeks.

It was a pity, but that was the way it was. At least they sometimes had a lot of fun when he came back. At least he sometimes brought strange things, or even people. Sometimes, it drove their mother up the wall . . .

Two hours later, the house was quiet, and a bit unhappy. The removal men had gone, John Sugden had gone, and their father had just driven down to the yard to pick up the wagon he had to take to Aberdeen, and then across to Glasgow, then down to Hull before returning to Manchester early in the week.

Before he had kissed them all goodbye, there had been a family meeting. The kids had had to stop messing about (they called it working) and put on their solemn faces.

'Listen,' Dad had said. 'The firm's sent me away, and Arthur's let us down.'

'The cowboy,' muttered Sam.

'Since we've moved in, we've discovered a fair few things the people who sold us the house didn't mention.'

'What?' asked Springy.

'Too thick to notice,' said Sam. 'Like the water

heater's bust, and the kitchen drain's blocked, and – '

Her father interrupted.

'Sam, why don't you put a sock in it, love? I haven't got all night.'

Sam flashed him a dirty look.

'Only trying to help.'

'Good. Because for the next two days, that's what you'll be doing. And if I hear reports when I come back that you haven't worked like madmen – I'll murder you, right?'

Then there had been a list of things that had to be done, and things that had gone wrong. Not just the heater, and the drain, but the rooms left dirty, the cooker not working properly, an electric light switch that gave you a shock if you touched it – all sorts.

It wasn't until half an hour after his father had left, and they'd had a cup of tea, that Springy dared confess it: the upstairs lavatory wouldn't flush, either.

'Oh well,' said Mum, tiredly. 'At least there's another one. We'll sort everything out in the morning.'

So instead of settling in next day, they worked. Instead of exploring the house and choosing their favourite rooms, they got to know the place at the end of a hoover tube, or over a

yellow duster as they scrubbed and rubbed away at filthy mantelpieces. Springy unloaded two cases of kitchen equipment and found shelves for it, while Sam (who was less of a wimp when it came to nasty smells) put on rubber gloves and cleaned the drain out with a piece of bendy tubing she found in the tumbledown shed.

Their mother emptied boxes, put up curtains, washed surfaces, arranged furniture, tried to make a meal on the cooker but had to give up, cursed the fact that she could only get hot water by using the small electric kettle, and shouted at them when they moaned.

Springy and Sam did get out once, at about six o'clock that evening. It was after they had sworn to their mother that they would drop dead if they did not eat something other than two-day-old cheese sandwiches. She looked at first as if she did not care.

Then she sat down on a chair and rubbed a dirty hand across her face, leaving a big black mark.

'You're right,' she said. 'I'm being daft. Of course we've got to eat. But what, and where from? We don't know the place at all.'

'There'll be a fish and chip shop,' said Sam. 'And there's a curry takeaway just round the corner, I saw it from the removal van. Just give us the money and put the kettle on. We won't take long.'

Mum wasn't sure about letting them out alone until they knew the area better, but they pointed out they could hardly get lost in the middle of a city on a busy Saturday evening in summer.

Anyway, she was exhausted. She gave in.

'I can't go myself,' she said. 'Not until we've got someone in to mend the front door. I suppose the removal men must have pushed it too far back, it's off its hinges.'

The area they'd come to live in was terrific. Their road was quiet, with two synagogues and a mosque, as well as a Catholic church and the tennis club, which had a snazzy tree-lined drive. Just around the corner were pubs, and shops, and restaurants of almost every type. Compared with their old home, it was fantastic.

'How about Greek?' asked Sam. 'That's my favourite takeaway. I'm going to have a mixed kebab with lots of chilli relish.'

Springy had a doner, and they got a shish and a mince for Mum, who had an appetite like a horse. They had enough left over for three tins of coke. Soon they were sitting in the jungle of the back garden in the late sunshine, eating and drinking hungrily.

'We haven't done too badly,' said Springy, with his mouth full of pitta bread and salad. 'We've cleared a lot away, and we haven't bust anything.'

'You haven't even blocked up any more lavs,' said Sam, nastily. 'Although there's still time, I suppose. *I've* unblocked a drain.'

Mum, however, did not seem very happy with the progress they'd made.

'You've worked well, kids,' she said. 'I must admit it. But there's so much to do. We won't even be able to sleep tonight until I've barred the front door up. It's crazy. We've worked all day, and we're still in chaos. How we're *ever* going to get straight enough to invite people in, I just haven't got the foggiest.'

At that moment, the front door bell rang. Before Mum had recovered from the surprise, Springy and Sam had raced through the kitchen and along the passage, their kebabs still in their hands.

It was an old man. Quite a strange old man. He smiled at them.

'Hallo,' he said. 'I'm Uncle Jock.'

'Uncle Jock?' said Sam. 'Whose Uncle Jock?'

The old man showed a mouthful of bent teeth in a broader grin.

'Well,' he said. 'Everybody's I suppose. Can I come in?'

It was Springy's turn to speak.

'Come in? Why?'

The eyes, under bushy white eyebrows, twinkled.

'Because I live here,' said Uncle Jock.

3 · The Mystery Room

Springy and Sam were flabbergasted.

'Oh,' said Sam, after a time. 'I can feel my mind boggling. What did you say again?'

The old man smiled. To him, the whole thing seemed like a very good joke.

'I said,' he repeated, 'can I come in? My name's Uncle Jock and I live here.'

'Mm,' said Sam. 'That's what I thought you said.'

Springy scratched his forehead.

'It is a boarding house,' he said. 'Or it was, anyway.'

'And it's going to be again, as soon as we get it straight,' added Sam. 'Yes.'

The old fellow tapped at the front door with a knobbly hand.

'That will need fixing for a start,' he said. 'It's off its hinges. Very dangerous, a glass door with the wood split like that. The glass could drop out any time.'

Springy pushed the door gingerly. He could see that Uncle Jock was right.

'Dad's been called away,' he said. 'He's a lorry driver. You'd better come in.'

At that moment, Mum called from the kitchen.

'Who is it, kids? Do you need me?'

'We're all right,' shouted Sam. 'Won't be a second. We've got a visitor.'

Uncle Jock certainly walked through the door as if he knew the place. More, in fact, as if he owned it. Springy and Sam stopped on the step for a second as he went along the passage. They had a funny feeling they might have done something wrong.

'He's a bit weird,' hissed Springy. 'Aren't his clothes funny?'

Uncle Jock was a very small man, but his trousers were big – too big for his legs. They flapped around his ankles as he walked, making a noise. He wore sandals with socks underneath them, but the socks had holes in. Both his big toes stuck out and wiggled. On his top half he had a yellow tee shirt and a holey jumper with no sleeves.

His lined, white-whiskery face was smiling and friendly, with a wide, flattish nose. On top of all, he wore a hat with the brim turned down,

like a baby's sunhat, only made of tartan cloth.

'He's something like a tramp,' whispered Sam.

As Uncle Jock reached the kitchen door, Mrs Price came out of it. She looked very tired, with her face pale. She stopped, surprised and put out.

'Who are you?' she said. Her voice was brisk, and not at all friendly.

'They call me – ' began the old man. But Sam interrupted him.

'He's Uncle Jock,' she said. 'We found him on the doorstep. He lives here.'

There was a little pause.

Springy added: 'So he says.'

Mother's face began to get angry. When she was tired she lost her temper very easily. Springy and Sam, who were used to it, got ready to run and hide. Springy wondered if they should warn the man.

'Uncle Jock?' said Mrs Price at last. 'That's not good enough. Who are you really, and why have you come into my house? How dare you?'

The old man said quietly: 'I was invited, ma'am. By the children. Not that it was their fault, you understand. This is my home.'

Sam said cleverly: 'If you live here, why did you ring the bell? Why didn't you just walk in?'

'Why don't you have a key, in any case?' said

Springy.

'You two shut up,' said Mum. 'This is nothing to do with you.'

But Uncle Jock looked at them seriously.

'You're wise children. I did not use my key or walk in out of politeness. Any fool could see The Kerry has changed hands. It's a great pity I was not told.'

Mum blew her top.

'*You* weren't told!' she snapped. 'What about me! Some old tramp turns up on my kitchen step and says he lives here! It's ridiculous!'

Springy and Sam both blushed. Maybe Uncle Jock was a bit scruffy, but to call him 'some old tramp' to his face! They did not dare tell their mother off, though.

Uncle Jock remained calm.

'I may look a little ragged, ma'am,' he said. 'But I have been travelling. My other clothes are in my room. I was expecting to bath and change.'

'Look,' said Mrs Price. 'I've had just about enough of today. The place is a tip, the heating doesn't work, the cooker's on the blink, and now you turn up. Just get out, will you? Go away.'

Springy, to be polite, said: 'You couldn't have a bath, Uncle Jock. There's no hot water. And the lav's blocked up.'

'That was Springy,' said Sam. 'He's an idiot.

He's my twin. I'm Sam.'

Uncle Jock was surprised. Most people were when they found out.

'Twins,' he said. 'But you're not like each other at all. Why, Springer's got red hair like a Scots lass, and Sam's is jet black.'

The children laughed.

'No no,' said Sam. '*I'm* Sam. It's short for something awful. And he's called Springy, not Springer.'

'I'm not a spaniel,' said Springy.

'He's bone idle,' said Sam. 'He needs a pointed stick up the backside, Dad says. To get him going. That's why he's called Springy. It's a joke.'

'Oh,' said Uncle Jock. 'Irony. I understand.'

Mother was still standing there, too tired to interfere, too tired to keep her anger boiling. She spoke.

'Look, Mister,' she said. 'I bought this boarding house empty, although it's meant to be ready furnished and running. I was conned, fair enough. But I did *not* buy any strange old men who claim to live here. For a start there are no rooms with anything in them, and secondly I'm not mad.'

'I live in the second attic, ma'am. I have a key here that will fit it.'

'There is no second attic,' said Mum. 'There is one attic, which contains a broken exercise

bicycle and a snooker table with three legs. Now will you please go away, before I call the police.'

For the children, it was a nasty moment. Anything could happen. All that did, was that the old man pulled a key from his pocket and held it up.

'I can assure you I am not telling stories, ma'am. The door is behind the top airing cupboard. The attic is very small, as is the rent. It suits an old sailor very well.'

Mrs Price looked at her watch.

'It's past my children's bed times,' she said. 'I'm tired and I have to barricade the door. I'll count to ten, and then I'll call the police.'

The old man sighed.

'Very well,' he said. 'I am the last person in the world to cause anybody any pain. I will go.'

As he walked down the passage, the children felt awful. But they did not dare to argue, or even to comment. Their mother calm could sometimes be worse than their mother raging. Ten seconds later, the front door was jerked screechily as far as it would close. Uncle Jock was gone.

Springy said: 'I suppose we can't look for the mystery attic, can we Mum?'

They could not.

4 · Cries in the Night

By Monday morning, things were beginning to look just a little better. The two children and their mother had spent the whole of Sunday working hard, and most of the basic arranging had been done.

All the right chairs and tables were in the right rooms, all the curtains were up, and the kitchen was ready to cook in − except that the cooker could not be trusted to stay alight.

Best of all was the announcement at the breakfast table that there would be no school for Springy and Sam today.

'You can't go to school without breakfast,' said Mum, 'and you can't have breakfast without a cooker. If the milk had come you could have had cereal, but it hasn't. I see neither of you has drunk your nice black tea!'

It was good to hear her joking about things again, although the situation really wasn't all that funny. They'd asked a milkman on Saturday to deliver, but he hadn't. In fact, if it hadn't been for all the takeaways in the district, they'd have starved to death on Sunday.

Mum seemed to think at first that she might have an argument on her hands about keeping them away from their new school on their first day, but she was wrong. Both the children were relieved.

'It's not that we don't like school,' said Springy. 'But it's a bit scary, isn't it? What if they don't have a good chess club?'

Sam laughed at her brother.

'Never mind boring old chess. Do they have a swimming team? Miss Malwin said that if I train hard I could be in the championship. She said Lapwing were always top of the schools' swimming league.'

'It's a good school, is what I've heard,' said Mrs Price. 'That's one of the reasons we moved here.'

The sun was shining brightly through the open back door, and birds were twittering noisily in the jungle. Funny, thought Sam, that she had heard her mother crying in her bedroom on Saturday night. Even last night there'd been suspicious sounds, although neither she nor her brother had been sure.

It had made them nervous to hear her crying, but they understood the reasons. Lying in sleeping bags on the bare boards of a dirty downstairs room wasn't exactly their idea of fun, either. One of today's tasks was to sort out proper rooms – with real beds in!

'Right,' said their mother. 'Let's start. I've got a list of things I've got to do down at the shops, and the cleaning lady from the agency's due soon. You two sort yourselves out while I phone the plumber and the Gas Board.'

Springy grinned at her.

'Do you know, Mum,' he said. 'I think you must feel better. You haven't moaned once about the panelling in this room!'

Sam groaned.

'Don't *remind* her,' she said.

Mrs Price made a face. She glanced at the dark, saggy panels. They really did make the breakfast room seem miserable.

'They're everywhere,' she said. 'The whole place has been decorated by a caveman. But first things first. Today, I think we'll get on top of it. Today, I think everything's going to go all right.'

But it wasn't. Two rings on the telephone before Sam leapt to it were the first blow. From there, things went downhill . . .

It was the cleaning agency. They were very

sorry, but the person Mrs Price had booked could not come in. No, they did not have anybody else. Would next week do?

Mum tried not to lose her temper. When she had put the phone down, she looked up plumbers in the Yellow Pages. But none of them replied, except one answering device. Mr Riley, it said, was on holiday. Please leave a message after the tone . . . The Gas Board were very sympathetic about the cooker, but they said they could not come till Thursday. Now if it had been a leak . . . Mrs Price could not even get a carpenter to look at the front door.

'Oh,' said Springy, sadly. 'Without a carpenter, we won't be able to open up the mystery attic either. I *did* want to have a peep inside.'

It was the wrong thing to mention, because Mum was fed to the back teeth with the mystery attic, and had forbidden them to even rattle the doorknob until their father got back from his job. She chased them angrily down into the cellars to sort out the electric fires and empty more boxes. All the growing jollity of ten minutes before had gone completely.

Springy and Sam had explored the upstairs area early on Sunday morning, and it had not taken them long to find Uncle Jock's 'secret' door.

As he had said, it was beside the airing cupboard, and it looked hardly any bigger. Painted brown and green, the door was like the entrance to a dwarf's den in a magic wood.

'It's a good job he's so small,' they had told their mother. 'It must be tiny in there. Can we try and break the lock?'

She had shooed them back to work, as she had today. Now, slaving in the cellars, they heard her at the top of the steps.

'I'm going out,' she said. 'I won't be very long, and I'm going to creep back when I come. If I catch you two not working, there'll be trouble. I mean it.'

Her voice was miserable. Springy and Sam looked at each other. They listened in silence until they heard the screech of the broken front door.

'Sam,' said Springy. 'I'm bored with this. I've got an idea.'

'You're mad,' his sister replied. 'And anyway, we're meant to be being good. What is it?'

Five minutes later, the two of them stood in the breakfast room, ready to start. They had put on their oldest jeans, and they had laid some dirty sheets over the table and the crockery cupboards. Springy had a claw hammer in his hand, and Sam was carrying a long screwdriver.

'I'm sure she'll be pleased, actually,' said Springy, although he wasn't sure at all. 'She ought to be. And look, the corner's hanging off already.'

'It does depress her,' agreed Sam, although she was nervous, too. 'If we pull it off and chuck it in the garden, the wall will only need cleaning down. The whole room will look different. Light, and airy, and bigger.'

They stood on chairs to get at the top of the gloomy brown panelling, and they had to prise and tug for quite a while before it started to peel off. It was plywood, covered in dark paper, and there were only a few thin nails keeping it in place.

'This is good,' said Springy, more cheerfully. 'It's probably already painted or wallpapered underneath, and we can easily run the hoover over the carpet afterwards.'

But almost as soon as the panelling began to tear away, the doubts and worries came flooding back. The thing was, that every time they pulled it an inch or so farther from the wall, great puffs of black and dirty dust flew out. Also, pieces of plaster, some of them quite big, kept falling off. They hit the mantelpiece, or broke on the radiators. The mess was starting to look alarming.

'Sam,' said Springy, after a while. 'I wish we

could stop. I don't think this is going according
to plan, you know. I don't think – '

With a sudden loud crack, the panelling split
from top to bottom. It went so fast, that
Springy, who was holding the upper edge and
standing on a chair, fell over backwards. Sam
slipped sideways, pulling her part of the plywood
right off the fireplace with a tearing sound.

Crash, went Springy, onto the table. The
table shot sideways and knocked the television
off its legs with another bang. Six plates slid
from underneath the dust sheet and smashed on
the floor.

'Heck,' wailed Sam, holding on to a piece of panelling. 'It's going to fall. Oh, Springy! The whole lot's coming down!'

There was a slipping, tumbling noise as piles of old, loose plaster fell off the front of the chimney breast. The panelling collapsed into the room, its corner breaking the glass front of a crockery cabinet. A cloud of filthy dust rose to the ceiling, then slowly fell.

The mess was horrendous. Quietly, almost silently, the door opened.

Mum stood there, looking in. Her mouth was wide open in horror.

5 · Saved by the Bell

Springy was lying on the floor, half covered in a sheet, and Sam was standing gaping. She was just trying to gasp out an explanation when the front door bell went.

'We were only trying to help, Mum,' she was saying. 'We thought that – '

Ring, went the bell. Springy, moving faster than he had for years, was on his feet and away down the passage like greased lightning. Sam was not far behind.

'Stephen!' roared their mother. 'Samantha! Come back into this room! Immediately!'

But Springy and Sam were on the doorstep. It was Uncle Jock. He was not smiling. He was not alone.

'Is your mother in, kids?' he began. Then he saw Mrs Price emerging from the breakfast room. He saw her face.

A less brave man would have turned and run

at this point. In fact, Springy and Sam thought it was stupid, not brave, to stay. But Uncle Jock did. He did not smile, but he did not go.

Mrs Price, this time, was not quiet angry, she was shouting mad. She was so mad, that a lot of what she said did not make sense, especially to Uncle Jock and the woman who stood silently beside him. Mrs Price was roaring.

She roared about what a pair of awful children she had, she roared about how she could not trust them to breathe, even, she roared about houses being vandalised and kitchens being wrecked, she roared about what their father would do to them when he returned, she even roared about what she would do to *him* for having gone away in the first place. She roared.

Then she turned her guns on Uncle Jock. The police were on their way, she lied, he had no right to be there, she stormed, and she wanted his rent book back immediately if he'd ever had one, which she doubted. And who, she wanted to know finally, was *that*?!

Springy and Sam gaped. It had been quite a good performance, even for their Mum with a full head of steam up. For themselves, they were very glad indeed that Uncle Jock was there. *And* the woman called 'that'. Because otherwise, they'd probably have been boiling in a pot by now . . .

When Mrs Price had run down, Uncle Jock spoke – as always, quietly and with dignity.

'Madam,' he said. 'I am truly sorry to trouble you at such a trying time. I have not come, as it happens, to cause you pain, grief, worry or woe, but quite the opposite, I hope. May I introduce you to Mrs Hilda Bagshaw?'

Would Mum jump on her? Would she tear her limb from limb and throw away the pieces? The children could hardly wait.

Mrs Hilda Bagshaw had not said a word so far. Nor had her face changed from the quiet, placid smile it had worn when the children had run to answer the bell. Now she spoke.

'I'm pleased to meet you, Mrs Price,' she said.

'It is Mrs Price, isn't it, love? That's what the neighbours say. Oh, I'm a cleaner, by the way, the best in West Didsbury, though I says it as shouldn't. I did for the last lot – mucky beggars they were – and I'll do for you as well. If you want me to, of course.'

'A cleaner!' said Sam, excitedly. 'That's just what we *need*. How did you *know*, Uncle Jock?'

Mrs Price's voice was faint.

'It's not just a cleaner I need,' she said. 'I think a gin would help. But if you cleaned for the last lot, Mrs Bagshaw – why is it such a filthy mess?'

Mrs Bagshaw pursed her lips.

'Mean,' she said. 'Ooh, you wouldn't believe how mean they were. And mucky. Have you seen the garden – well! And they wouldn't let me touch a thing when they moved. They said that was *your* problem. Ooh, they were 'orrible.'

'And I,' said Uncle Jock, 'can vouch for that. Mrs Bagshaw and Trannie are the best team for miles around.'

'Trannie?'

Mrs Bagshaw was a short, fat, dumpling of a woman. Beside her ankles were a big black plastic bag, a mop bucket and mop, and a square object, covered with a cloth.

'It's a budgie cage,' said Springy. 'Have you got a budgie?'

Like a magician, Mrs Hilda Bagshaw whipped the cloth off. On a perch, seeming to blink in the sunshine, was a bright green bird.

'Trannie,' she said.

The budgie jerked its head and squawked. Then it said: 'Picadilly, two six one. The success of the North West!'

'He's noisy,' said Mrs Bagshaw, cheerfully. 'But he's not as noisy as a real radio, and you can't get pop on him, so that's a blessing, isn't it?'

'Picadilly Radio,' shrieked Trannie. 'Umberto, where the devil are you, lad?'

Uncle Jock, seeing Mum's face, said to the cleaning lady: 'I'd cover him up if I was you, Hilda. You haven't got the job yet.'

Mother smiled.

'Uncle Jock,' she said (and the children gaped – she'd called him Uncle Jock, and she wasn't shouting), 'you've got the right idea. Thank you very much for bringing Mrs Bagshaw round. But I'm afraid you *still* can't stay.'

Uncle Jock nodded.

'Ma'am,' he said. 'It's your house, and I respect your wishes. But there is the small matter of a broken door, I believe. Plus the heating not working, and the gas cooker playing up, not to mention some trouble with the toilets. Correct me if I'm wrong, but you won't have managed to find a builder or a plumber yet?'

'They wouldn't come,' chipped in Springy. 'The Gas Board said we've to wait till Thursday.'

'In my room,' said Uncle Jock. 'Correction. In what was *once* my room, but which I shall clear of everything the moment you give me permission, I have tools. I have woodworking tools, and I have plumbing tools. I have saws and blowlamps, spanners and planes. I am highly skilled in both departments, believe me.'

With shocking suddenness, there was a terrific crash from the breakfast room. Trannie, underneath his cloth, shrieked. Everybody looked down the passage at the cloud of dust and plaster that was drifting towards them.

'I have also been a builder in my time,' said Uncle Jock. 'It sounds to me as if your chimney breast has just collapsed.'

There was a silence. Springy and Sam thought their mother was going to get at them again.

'We only tried to help,' said Springy. 'We wanted to make it nice and light for you.'

'The panelling just fell down,' said Sam. 'We didn't think everything else would come as well.'

Mrs Hilda Bagshaw ran a finger through some of the plaster dust that was settling all around.

'Come on, Trannie,' she said. 'Let's get to work.'

6 · A Military Operation

When the children led the way into the breakfast room, the feeling they'd had that the worst was over disappeared very fast indeed.

'Oh my gosh,' said Sam. 'Don't let Mum in! Quick!'

It was silly, and it was too late. Mrs Price was just behind them. She gave a gasp.

The breakfast room was incredible. It was like a house that had been pulled down, or hit by a bomb. The air was so thick with dust, that they could hardly see from one side of it to the other.

'Where's the furniture?' squeaked Springy.

It was underneath the chimney breast. Underneath about four hundred old and broken bricks, jumbled together with tons of concrete and plaster. Part of the ceiling had been pulled down as well. What chairs you could see were broken, sticking out at funny angles from the rubble.

'What did you *do*?' asked their mother. Her

voice was croaky and odd. Sam shot a glance at her to see if she was crying.

But Mum was not. She just looked pale, and totally shocked.

'Months,' she said. 'Oh heck, it'll take *months*. We'll never get the people in.'

Springy and Sam could only agree. Springy looked around to see if he could find anything for his Mum to sit on, but he couldn't.

Uncle Jock, crowded into the doorway behind the family, took over.

'Months?' he said. 'Nonsense. You've never seen us work, has she, Mrs Bagshaw? Turn your Trannie on. Let's have some jollity on the scene!'

Mrs Bagshaw twitched the cover off the cage.

'It's a bit dusty,' she said. 'I hope it doesn't make him cough.'

Trannie hopped about, seeming pleased to see the light again.

'Susie Mathis — Good afternoooooooon!' he sang. 'Let me out, Mrs Bagshaw! Nobody does it better!'

To Springy and Sam's surprise, Mrs Hilda Bagshaw bent down and unclipped the budgie's cage door. He hopped onto the sill, then fluttered off down the passage.

'The front door's open!' shrieked Sam.

'It's competition time,' chirped Trannie. Then

he said, over and over again: 'Sweenie! Sweenie! Sweenie! Sweenie! Sweenie!'

'Listen to the Salford accent,' said Mrs Bagshaw fondly. 'Sweenie's his favourite DJ. Daft little bird!'

'But won't he fly away?' asked Springy. The cleaning lady smiled.

'He's too old for that sort of caper,' she said. 'Susie Mathis works for BBC now. That's how old he is.'

Uncle Jock, sensing that mother had had just about all she could stand, began to organise things.

'Sam,' he said to Springy. 'Go and put the kettle on. Make sure it's not full of dust, and rinse out some mugs for tea. Springy,' he went on, to Sam, 'find me the Yellow Pages, and look up Skip Hire, quick. Can you read?'

'My name's Sam not Springy,' said Sam. 'Can you see?'

'Don't be rude,' said Mrs Price. 'Skip hire? What for?'

'To hire a skip,' said Uncle Jock. 'I may be small, Mrs P, but I'm very strong. Me and your two sprogs will have the rubble out before dinnertime. Then we'll get down to the serious business.'

'I've kissed Curly Shirley,' shrieked Trannie. He fluttered out through the front door into the sunshine.

Uncle Jock and Mrs Bagshaw between them organised The Big Clean Up like a military operation. Mother was hustled into the back kitchen to find extra mops, cloths and buckets, then she was pushed and prodded upstairs by the cleaning lady to the very top of the house.

'You and me, being ladies, will do the light work first,' she said. 'We'll clean all the muck and rubbish from the top to the bottom, until we meet the muck and rubbish downstairs. Then we'll have a cup of tea and a think, like.'

'We,' said Uncle Jock to Springy and Sam, 'will fill the skip when it comes, and strip off the rest of this panelling. Then tomorrow we'll get some sand and cement delivered, and a bag or two of plaster, and some Thistle Finish.'

Mother, halfway up the bottom stairs, was bemused.

'What for, Uncle Jock?' she asked. 'I mean . . . well . . . what for?'

He laughed.

'To rebuild the chimney breast, of course. I've looked at the bricks. They're all right, and there's more in the garden. When we've cleared, we'll start from scratch. Then we plaster it and finish it. Day after tomorrow we can paper, if you like. Or maybe you'll just emulsion it?'

'The day after *tomorrow*?'

Uncle Jock looked doubtful.

'Is that too long? I might be able to finish sooner, but my labourers are a shade on the small side, aren't they? That might slow me down.'

Mrs Price could not believe it.

'I meant it was so *quick*,' she said. 'Can you *really* do it?'

Mrs Hilda Bagshaw prodded her with a broom.

'Not if you keep mithering him,' she said. 'Come on, Mrs P. Let's get doing.'

'While we're waiting for the skip, I'll show Springy and Sam how to get the heating going,' said Uncle Jock. 'It's a valve on the blink. It's always happening.'

In the next hour, the children learned more about the workings of a house than they ever expected to in their lives. They saw the insides of a gas central heating boiler, they were shown cisterns and ballcocks and fuses, they were told about thermostats and pilot lights. Both of them turned the faulty valve on and off three times to see how to do it in future.

Uncle Jock would not let them touch the insides of the cooker, but he showed them the problem there, as well.

'In the trade we call it the Rice Pudding Factor,' he said. 'Someone boils some rice or some milk or something, and it spills over and gets into the gas jets. Then it hardens up with the heat – and bingo! The cooker doesn't work. Now – where's that darning needle?'

Upstairs, which they visited every now and then to see if Mum was all right (and to listen to Radio Picadilly on the small green Trannie!) they learned more about the area they'd moved to, from Mrs Bagshaw.

They learned of all the different colours and races who lived there, of the students and the rich folk who jostled to get hold of the enormous old houses that could be turned into flats – expensive or cheap – of the exotic food and music that could be sampled just a stone's throw from their front door.

'It's changed,' said Mrs Hilda Bagshaw. 'When I was a little girl here us poor kids didn't dare walk down this street, it was so posh. Now the whole world lives here. It's lovely.'

Without their realising it, it was late. Springy and Sam, black and exhausted from filling the skip with rubble, were brought to their senses by a shriek from Mrs Bagshaw, from upstairs.

'Is that the time! Glory be! Ernie will be home for tea, and me still here! Oh, Mrs Price! You never should have let me chatter on!'

The dumpy cleaning lady, whistling for her budgie, bounced and waddled down the flights of stairs. Dirty-faced and panting, she pulled on her coat and bundled Trannie into his travelling home. Uncle Jock stood at the breakfast room door.

'Gone six,' he said. 'Perhaps I'd better clean up and go and find a café.'

Mother smiled.

'You'll do no such thing, Uncle Jock,' she said. 'You'll eat with us.'

Yippee.

7 · Mother Gets Tough

As the kids ran round to the Greek takeaway, they talked about the fun they were having. The sight of a few children of about their own age, who had obviously been stuck in school all day, made it seem that much better.

'Had your look?' shouted Sam, at one boy. She added to her brother: 'Anyone'd think he'd never seen a girl before.'

Springy laughed.

'I doubt if he's seen one as dirty as you,' he said. 'We probably won't get served in the takeaway.'

True, they got some more funny looks, but they were given their food. The man behind the counter, whom they already knew was called Christos, recognised them.

'Hallo,' he said. 'Been knocking down your house already?'

Two boys playing with the space invaders

machine in the corner were listening hard.

'Building it,' said Sam. 'A bit fell down this morning, and we've spent all day mending it.'

Springy, knowing that the boys must be in their year, added proudly: 'We couldn't go to school. It was meant to be our first day, too.'

'Oh,' said Christos. 'You want chilli relish or mustard?'

On the way home, Springy and Sam reckoned they'd have to do another full day's work at least on the house. They'd wake up Uncle Jock first thing and carry on with their new trade as builders.

'He's going to teach us to mix sand and cement,' said Springy. 'He says it's easy. I'd like to be a bricklayer, maybe, when I grow up. Or a brain surgeon.'

'He says plastering's more difficult,' said Sam. 'I bet I can learn it though. It helps, not being thick like you!'

They all sat round in the big front downstairs room eating their kebabs, and the children chattered on.

'What time shall we wake you in the morning, Uncle Jock?' asked Springy. 'Mum – we are having another day off school, aren't we?'

'We saw two boys in the takeaway,' said his sister. 'They were horrible.'

Their mother was looking at them, her shish by her open mouth. She was puzzled.

'How do you mean, wake him up?' she said. 'Where do you think he'll be?'

The children could hardly believe their ears.

'He'll be here,' said Sam, angrily. 'Won't you, Uncle Jock?'

'He's rebuilding the breakfast room,' said Springy. 'We all are. It'll take another day at least.'

'Anyway,' said Sam. 'He's been helping you. He's worked like a Trojan. You don't honestly mean to say you'd throw him out into the gutter!'

Uncle Jock let out a hoot of laughter.

'Kids, kids,' he said. 'Don't go silly. I'll stay with Mrs Bagshaw again. They've got a comfy sofa.'

'Sofa!' stormed Sam. 'It's ridiculous! Mum, you can't do it. We won't let you. Will we, Springy?'

Springy, who was less ready to fight than Sam, nodded cautiously.

'It's not right, Mum,' he muttered.

Mrs Price put down what was left of her kebab. She turned to Uncle Jock.

'I'm sorry,' she said. 'It's embarrassing, all this. They're too young to understand.'

'We are *not too young*!' yelled Sam. She was

red in the face.

Mum said quietly: 'You are too young, Samantha. There are such things as laws, you know. There are problems about rents, and sitting tenants, and conditions of letting, and so on.'

'I know,' said Sam. 'I've heard you talk about it to Dad, you boring pair of money-grubbers. You're afraid if you let Uncle Jock stay you won't be able to get rid of him!'

Springy was shocked.

'But we don't want to get rid of him,' he said.

'She does!' shouted Sam, pointing at Mum. 'She wants to get someone posher in! She wants to get a bigger rent!'

Jock stood up.

'Sam,' he said (and he got it right), 'I think you've said enough. Your mother and me know what's right and wrong, and we're not arguing.'

'It's wrong to throw you out!' said Sam. 'Just because you're not rich.'

He smiled.

'It's wrong to upset your mother,' he said. 'And although I am of very limited means, I doubt if your Mum and Dad are millionaires, either.'

'Very limited means?' said Springy. 'What does that mean?'

Sam turned to him.

'It means he's skint,' she said. 'And he can't live here any more. Oh! It makes me *sick*!'

She stormed out of the room. They heard doors slamming all over the house. They looked at each other.

'I'll stay with the Bagshaws like I said,' Uncle Jock told Springy. 'I'll be all right, honest. Come on – we'd better get back to work.'

They did, but it was not the same. Mum disappeared somewhere so that she did not have to be in the same room, and Sam did not help for ages. In fact, no one knew where she was.

Springy and Uncle Jock went on tidying, and filling the skip, but they worked much more slowly than before. Although they both thought hard, they could not really think of much to say.

Springy said: 'What's it *really* like at Mrs Bagshaw's? Doesn't Trannie drive you mad?'

Uncle Jock replied: 'It's not too bad, but her husband's a pain. He only talks about his job. All the time. That drives you up the wall.'

'Oh,' said Springy. 'What does he do?'

'He works at the sewage farm. He's not only boring, but he pongs as well. But he's a nice enough old feller.'

Sam came back at last, and joined in: 'Can she cook?' she said. 'She doesn't look as if she can.'

Springy thought she was being daft.

'You can't tell if someone can cook by looking at them,' he said.

'Maybe you can,' said Uncle Jock. 'Anyway, Sam's quite right. She can't even boil a spud without wrecking it. It's worse grub than I used to get on the tramp ships in the bad old days.'

At nine o'clock, Mum came to the breakfast room door. She seemed depressed, and ashamed. She would not look Uncle Jock in the eye.

'Time for bed, you kids,' she said. 'But before you go, get in the bath. I've sorted out some clothes for you.'

Sam said nastily: 'If it wasn't for Uncle Jock, we wouldn't have any hot water, would we?'

'Shush up, Sam,' said Uncle Jock. He turned to mother. 'Mrs Price. Would it be all right if I went up to the attic for five minutes? I need to get some things.'

Mother blushed.

'Of course,' she said.

'Well *we're* going too,' said Sam. She grabbed Springy by the dirty hand and pulled him towards the passage. As she passed, she glared at her Mum.

'Because we don't particularly want to be with *you*,' she said.

8 · The Wonderful Attic

As the children walked down the passageway towards the front door – and the bottom of the stairs – they noticed that the sky had darkened outside. Not just because night was falling, either. There were big drops of rain beginning to plop down. It matched their black mood perfectly.

Uncle Jock, though, did not appear to be fed up. As the three of them trudged up the thirty-four steps in two separate flights, he was actually whistling. It seemed a daft time to be cheerful, to them.

'What's the matter with you?' asked Sam, grumpily. 'You're just about to be turned out of your own home, and you seem to be enjoying it.'

Uncle Jock laughed.

'It's summer,' he said. 'I can put up with Hilda Bagshaw's cooking. I can think of worse things to happen to a man.'

They stopped outside the little brown and green door. It really was quite tiny and odd.

'Anyway,' he added. 'I'm looking forward to seeing my room again. I like it.'

He fished around in the pocket of his big trousers for quite a few seconds. A knife came out, and a lot of string, and some elastic bands. It was like a kid's pocket, not a man's. Finally two keys appeared, on a circle of fishing twine. A front door key and a fat, old-fashioned one.

'There,' said Uncle Jock. 'The key to Aladdin's Cave.'

Small as he was, even he had to stoop to get to the lock. He grinned, and twisted the old key rapidly to the left.

'It's none too tidy,' he said. 'But you won't care about that, will you?'

As Uncle Jock pushed gently, the old door creaked. It was perfect, as if they were entering a haunted house. Inside, although there was a small window, it was dark.

'Now,' he said. 'Let's get some light on the subject.'

For a moment, in the glare of the naked bulb hanging from the ceiling, the children were blinded.

Then, as her vision came back, Sam gave a little squeak.

Facing her, across the single bed, was a very
ancient man, dressed up in a blue sailor's jersey
and a coat. He was *very* thin.

'Blimey Moses!' yelped Springy. 'It's a
skeleton!'

Sam blinked. She saw that it was. It was
grinning hideously at her, from underneath a
knitted bobble cap.

'That's Captain Ahab,' said Uncle Jock. 'He
came from Cardiff a hundred years ago, and he's
been looking for Wales ever since.'

He chuckled as if he'd made a joke, but the
children were too fascinated by his room to care.

'It's fan*tas*tic!' breathed Springy. 'It's a

treasure cave! It's wonderful!'

'What's that?' asked Sam, pointing. 'Is that another of your sailor friends?'

'Shipmates is the word,' said Uncle Jock. He pushed some cardboard boxes to one side so that he could get into a corner. 'No, there's no one in there. It's a diving suit.'

Sam wanted to be a diver when she grew up, but she had only ever seen pictures of this type of suit. It was a man-shaped canvas thing, with gigantic lead boots, a huge bright copper helmet, and lots of tubes dangling all around it.

'Look at its *hands*,' she said. 'Ooh, they're like a pound of sausages!'

'Two pounds,' said Springy. 'One to each arm. Fancy having to pick things up with gloves like that on.'

'Better than having your fingers eaten off by eels,' said Uncle Jock. 'Hey! Mind where you're rooting!'

Sam had almost disappeared into a pile of assorted items in one corner. She emerged, red-faced, with three extremely peculiar-looking dolls. They were black-faced, with pointed heads and painted beards, and they had long thin sticks attached to their hands and bodies.

'What are they? Are they dolls? What do they do?'

'They're Balinese puppets,' said Uncle Jock. 'They operate them behind silken screens, so that you see the shadows move.'

'Just the shadows? But the dolls are lovely!'

He laughed.

'The shows are like magic,' he said. 'Ah, those nights on the islands. I wish I was young again.'

Springy said: 'Have you been everywhere? In the world?'

Uncle Jock laughed again.

'Everywhere with a deep-water port,' he said. 'I started in Montego Bay and I sailed the Seven Seas.' He sighed. 'I thought I'd finally come to anchor here.'

Springy noticed the sadness in his voice, but Sam was busy rooting again. She was uncovering a peculiar object from under a green and shiny cloth.

'Hey! Careful! You'll knock down the finest cathedral in the world!'

'But it's made of . . . matchsticks?'

'That's right. Eleven years I've been at that. Norwich Cathedral out of matchsticks, that was my ambition. It's got a lot slower lately, I can tell you.'

'Why?'

'Because I gave up smoking!'

There was more treasure in the room, much more. Tiny model trains and aeroplanes, jade and ivory figures, two elephants' feet – from the same elephant, according to Uncle Jock – some working steam engines, and chests of tools of every type, all oiled and polished and gleaming. In one corner was a workbench, and from the low, sloping ceiling hung more small tools for wood and metal.

'There's not much room to sit down, is there?' said Springy. 'And you haven't got a telly.'

'If I'm not working here I'm sleeping,' said Uncle Jock. 'Or reading. Why bother with sitting in an armchair and watching shadows on a screen?'

'Oh dear,' said Sam, remembering. 'Oh dear, Uncle Jock. I . . . Oh dear.'

Without asking, Springy knew what was in her mind. It was all over. Uncle Jock was going. All three of them grew very quiet.

'Ah well,' said the old man. 'Some of it will sell, I suppose. I doubt if I'll starve to death.'

'Some of it?' asked Springy. 'But all of it's worth a fortune, surely? You'll be rich!'

He shook his head.

'Junk,' he said. 'Treasure to you and me, but to grown-up people – junk. The diver's helmet might fetch a few quid, and the boots. But . . . '

'What about the skeleton?'

'Nah. Poor old Ahab's lost a leg, for a start. He'll end up on the scrapheap, like many another poor old sailorman.'

Sam was going red again. She was getting angry.

'We can't have it!' she snapped. 'Mum's just got no right. It's impossible!'

Uncle Jock touched her on the shoulder.

'Leave it, Sam,' he said. 'I know how you feel, but leave it. It's not your mother's fault, and in a way she's right.'

'Nonsense,' said Sam. 'If all this stuff's going to end up on the tip, how can she be right?'

Outside, there was an enormous crash of

thunder. Springy jumped.

'Right!' Sam told him. 'Downstairs, you. And back me up, Toad! We're going to have it out with Mum!'

Uncle Jock tried once more to stop her, then shrugged. As they rattled off down the attic stairs, he began to pack a bag.

Crash! went the kitchen door. Sam almost took it off its hinges. Springy, behind her, winced. He expected trouble. Mega-trouble.

But Mum was not alone. As Sam opened her mouth to launch into her, the children saw another woman there. A woman they did not know.

'Samantha,' said her mother, mildly. 'Do you have to break the door down? This is your new teacher, Mrs Jackson.'

9 · Home Truths

Like most children, Springy and Sam had heard wild stories of what could happen to you if you skipped school. For a moment, they thought the teacher was going to produce a cane or something and terrify them on the spot.

She was sitting on a wooden kitchen chair amid the chaos, and she did not look too worried by it. The mug in her hand was quite dirty, and the milk bottle on the table was covered in dust. Come to think of it, so was the kitchen table.

'I came round to see where you'd got to today,' she said. 'And to say Hello.'

Springy blurted out: 'But it's night. It's bed time.'

Mrs Jackson nodded.

'So it is,' she said. 'But who goes to bed on time when they've just moved into a new house? I thought I'd find you up.'

Sam eyed the teacher up and down. She

wasn't very big, and she did not appear particularly vicious.

'We couldn't come in today,' she said. 'We were much too busy.'

'Sam,' said her mother, half under her breath. The teacher raised her eyebrows. They were black, and quite bushy for a woman.

'Yes,' said Mrs Jackson. 'I can see you were. Do you always have this effect on things?'

'What?' said Sam. The teacher threw her hand out in a big gesture.

'The mess. The fallen-down brickwork. The sagging ceiling. Your mother tells me you and . . . er, Stephen, did it.'

Sam's temper flashed.

'That's not fair!' she said. 'We didn't!'

Springy said: 'Yes we did, Sam.' To the teacher he went on: 'But it was an accident. And my name's Springy, not Stephen. Unless I've been naughty, or something.'

A frown crossed Mrs Jackson's face.

'In my book,' she said, 'knocking down your mother's lovely new home would probably go under the heading of naughty.' She paused. 'Stephen.'

Springy went red, but Sam started to get nowty once more.

'Well it wasn't our fault, and we've worked like mad all day to put it right,' she said. 'And we're not coming to your stupid school tomorrow, either. So there!'

Mum stood up. She was pale and tired, as she had been ever since they'd moved. Too tired to rampage.

'You've said enough,' she told Sam. 'Get upstairs and get to bed, both of you. You can either bath now, or get up very early in the morning. Because you *are* going to school.'

Even Springy was shocked.

'We *can't*,' he wailed. 'We've got to rebuild the fire front. There's plastering to be done, and papering, and painting. It'll be *days*.'

Before Mum could speak, Mrs Jackson butted in.

'You're not doing it *yourselves*, are you? Goodgollygosh, Class K could certainly do with a couple of builders.'

'Of course they're not doing it themselves,' began Mum.

'We are,' snapped Springy. 'We're helping Uncle Jock. He says we're very good bricklayers.'

'Cherry and Pip can take some lessons from you,' said the teacher. Everyone looked at her, wondering what the heck. She made a face. 'They're the class hens,' she said. 'They can only lay eggs. Sorry, it was a joke.'

That's all we need, thought Springy and Sam together. A loony teacher. They shared the thought with a glance.

'Anyway,' said Springy. 'For once Sam's right. Until the breakfast room's done *at least*, we can't come to school. Even if we have to go to prison.'

'We mean it,' added Sam, watching the teacher's face with interest. 'It's *important*.'

Mrs Jackson had an unusual face. It was long and thinnish, with a big mouth that was never still. It was always making shapes, and little whistles and noises to go with her silly oaths, like 'Goodgollygosh'. She came out with another of them now.

'Hot maggots,' she said. 'You are a wild pair. I

can see I'll have some fun with you. Your mother says you're twins, and she ought to know, I suppose. Are you?'

Springy was going to answer properly, but Sam just snorted. She thought the teacher was wriggling out of it.

'We're not coming,' she said. 'And that's flat. So what do you say to that?'

Just then, though, Uncle Jock poked his head round the door, tartan hat first. He was carrying a bag, and he did not have a coat.

'I'm off then,' he said cheerfully. 'I'll see you in the morning, Mrs Price.'

The children were instantly ashamed. It looked as if they'd forgotten him. They'd raced downstairs to have a row with Mum, and they'd met this crazy teacher. Sam rushed over and grabbed his arm.

'You stay there,' she said. 'We haven't finished with her yet. We haven't even started.'

'He can't go,' said Springy. 'We've seen his room and it's not junk, it's treasure. It can't go on the scrapheap, and nor can Uncle Jock. If he leaves this house tonight – so do I!'

Mrs Jackson made a face of amazement at this.

'Whew,' she breathed. 'Jeepers b'jeep.'

'Anyway,' said Sam, 'he hasn't even got a coat, look. And it's pouring down outside. There's thunder and lightning.'

'Sam,' said Uncle Jock. 'Springy. Mrs Bagshaw only lives in the next street. I've told you. It's useless and I don't mind.'

'Well *we* do,' said Springy. He ran to his mother and glared at her. 'After all he's done for you,' he said. 'He's got a skip, he's cleaned the place up, he's rebuilding the rotten walls.'

'He's mended the heating, he's mended the cooker, he's unblocked the lav, even,' went on Sam.

'And his room's only a tiny little place and it's full of fantastic gear and stuff. A steam engine, and a diver's suit, and Norwich Cathedral made of matches. And he says you'll say it's junk and it'll end up on the tip, like him.'

They paused for breath. Mrs Jackson muttered: 'Treasure, eh? Mm.' Mother, overwhelmed, still had not spoken. Both she and Uncle Jock were embarrassed by the whole row, you could tell.

'What's more,' said Springy, 'Uncle Jock doesn't owe you *anything*, does he? You owe *him*. How much is he charging for all this work, eh? He's not a cowboy, like Uncle Arthur, is he? How much have you offered him?'

Nobody had thought of this before. It was a bombshell. Mrs Price, turning pink, threw a look at Uncle Jock. He was shaking his head vigorously.

'Out of order, Springy,' he said. 'Completely out of order, that. My services were offered in the name of friendship, free. Damsels in distress. You know.'

Sam snorted.

'Damsels in distress!' She almost spat the words out. 'Mum's kicking you into the rain and making you homeless all to make a few more measly quid and you call her a damsel in distress! If I'd been Saint George, I'd have helped the dragon eat her!'

Mum was now bright red. She looked at Mrs Jackson, almost helplessly.

'I'm sorry about all this,' she said. 'It's a problem that's come to me with the boarding house. The children don't understand what's going on, and they think I'm being heartless.'

'You are! You are!'

Uncle Jock would have no more of it.

'I'm off,' he said. 'Sam. Springy. Any more of this, and the deal's off. I'll hire new labourers. You won't work for me any more.'

They were bowled over.

'But we're on your side! We're fighting for your room.'

'And your treasure. And your health!'

'My *health*?' said Uncle Jock. '*Now* what are you talking about?'

'Oh never mind,' said Springy, crossly. 'It's the rain. You'll catch your death of cold.'

Uncle Jock started laughing. At first nobody else found anything funny. The room was tense. But after a few seconds, Sam began to giggle. Smiles appeared. Mum sat down, and Mrs Jackson stood up.

'If you're really going,' she said to Uncle Jock, 'I could give you a lift.'

'He isn't,' said Sam.

'Or we go too,' said Springy.

There was quite a pause. Mrs Price let out a sigh.

'What would you do with them, Mrs Jackson?' she said.

For a teacher, Mrs Jackson said a very peculiar thing.

'I think I'd flog them to within an inch of their lives,' she said. 'Then I'd hang them by the thumbs from a dungeon wall for a week.'

She nodded.

'That should sort 'em out.'

10 · Surprises for Dad

One of the best things about Springy and Sam's father was that his homecomings were terrific.

Although he was often tired, he never let it show too much. It was a rule of his never to shout at the kids because *he* was having a bad time.

He did not bring them presents, because that would have been ridiculous. He was away so often that he would have ended up bankrupt. But every now and again, out of the blue, he surprised them with something.

This time, though, it was Dad's turn to be surprised. He was.

Springy and Sam were working on the final papering of the breakfast room when they heard the front door bang (it closed now, properly). Then came the familiar shout.

'Jean! Anyone! I'm back!'

They dropped their brushes and the piece of

paper they had been getting ready to paste, and raced into the passageway.

'Dad! Dad! Yippee!'

Mr Price's head emerged from under a mountain of children to kiss his wife, who had walked more slowly from the kitchen, wiping her hands. He was coughing.

'What's this?' he said. 'You two are all covered in dust. Look at the state of your clothes!'

Springy and Sam giggled.

'Look at the state of the house,' said Springy. 'Haven't you noticed anything?'

Mr Price looked about him, then at his watch.

'And another thing,' he said. 'Why aren't you at school? Not been expelled already have you?'

From upstairs there was a squawk. A voice shrieked: 'Sweenie, Sweenie, Sweenie!'

'Picadilly Radio?' said Dad. 'Just what's going on?'

'Stereo one-oh-three,' shrieked the voice.

'I need a cup of tea,' said Dad.

The children weren't at school, they explained over steaming mugs, because their teacher had told them not to bother.

'What?' said Mr Price. 'But that's against the law!'

Mrs Price nodded.

'Not in front of the children, dear,' she said,

winking at them. 'She said not to make a song and dance about it. She seems a pretty odd teacher to me.'

'She's fantastic!' said Sam and Springy together. 'She's *great*!'

'Well,' said Dad. 'That's half the battle, I suppose. You never really liked your teachers at the last school, did you?'

'Mrs Jackson's got some brains,' said Springy. 'We're going to teach her bricklaying.'

'Painful,' said Dad. He jerked his head in surprise. 'Bricklaying!' he said. 'What do you two know about bricklaying?'

It took them twenty minutes to show him what they'd done to The Kerry, and a few minutes more to show him the valve that went wrong on the central heating, and the lavatory cistern that sometimes jammed. It took them even longer to convince him that they'd done the jobs themselves – or at least part of them.

'We're only labourers, really,' said Sam, with unusual modesty. 'We couldn't have done it on our own.'

'No,' replied Dad. 'I don't suppose you could. In fact, I would have thought *causing* damage was more your line.'

Mother nodded.

'The truth is out,' she said. 'Springy and Sam

did knock down the chimney breast. But to be fair, they've been a great help in putting everything to rights. Uncle Jock couldn't have done it without them.'

Dad was getting more and more confused.

'All right,' he said. 'Who's Uncle Jock?'

A flash of green, and Trannie had flown into the room.

'It's Young Cuddly Dave,' he squeaked. 'Timmy thinks you're past it!'

Dad shook his head.

'I probably am,' he said. 'And this is Uncle Jock's parrot, of course?'

'He's not a parrot, silly!' cried Sam. 'He's a budgie, and he's called Trannie because he thinks he's Picadilly Radio.'

'And he doesn't belong to Uncle Jock,' said Springy. 'He's Mrs Bagshaw's. She's the cleaner.'

'Jean,' said Mr Price. 'I need another cup of tea. I need an explanation.' He took his head in his hands. 'I wish I'd stayed on the road,' he said. 'Less mither.'

It was explained, slowly, over the next few minutes, and Mrs Hilda Bagshaw came downstairs to be introduced.

'I did for the last lot,' she said. 'Dirty devils they were, Mr Price. And I'll do for you and all.'

She bobbed her head, whistled for Trannie, and waddled off again.

'The upstairs is almost fit enough for pigs to live in now,' she said, over her shoulder. 'I know I shouldn't say it, but it's mainly thanks to me!'

Trannie, fluttering after her, added: 'Nobody does it better!'

The house had been changed about beyond recognition, Dad had to admit. The breakfast room was almost repapered, in white, which made it look bigger, and brighter, and nicer. The kitchen was spick and span, with pots bubbling on the cooker, and everything was in full working order.

'Amazing,' he said. 'When I left on Friday I thought it'd be six months. In fact, I thought your mother would have left me when I came back!'

'I very nearly did,' said Mum. 'And you'd have deserved it.'

'If it hadn't been for Uncle Jock she might have,' said Springy. 'It's him we ought to thank.'

The time had come.

'Enough,' said Dad. 'If someone doesn't tell me who this Uncle Jock is, I'll burst. And where the heck is he?'

Sam grinned.

'He's the lodger,' she said. 'The first. In fact, he sort of came with the house.'

'But for the moment,' said Springy, 'Mum doesn't charge him rent. Because he's doing all the building for us.'

'And he's skint.'

Father looked at mother across their heads.

'Oh, terrific,' he said. 'This is the new hard business woman, is it? This is the woman who's going to put the family on its feet? This is the woman who's going to earn the money for the little luxuries? Rent free!'

'That's not for long,' said Mrs Price. She laughed. 'But I won't be charging him a lot, when it comes to it. It's only a little attic room, and he is a bit short of cash.'

Sam said: 'Except his room's full of treasure.'

Springy added: 'Which is only really junk.'

'He's an old merchant seaman,' said Mum. 'He's smashing, Jeff. You'll like him.'

'Chance would be a fine thing, wouldn't it? Where is this mystery lodger?'

'He's at the hardware store. We needed some moulding for the breakfast room. To do the picture rail.'

They all heard the front door at the same moment.

'He's not,' said Sam. 'He's back.'

The children watched carefully and anxiously to see how the two men would get on. The tiny old fellow in the tartan hat and trampy clothes, and their tall, thin, clean father.

'Pleased to meet you, Cap'n,' said Uncle Jock. 'I hear you drive lorries.'

'I do,' said Dad. 'You're Uncle Jock?'

'That's what they call me. I drove lorries once. Antar. Tank transporter, in the war.'

'Wow,' said Dad. 'I'm not in heavy stuff, like that. I've just done a trip in an ERF. Gardner 240.'

'Good engine, the Gardner,' said Uncle Jock. He glanced at Springy and Sam. 'They're built just down the road,' he said. 'Patricroft, near Eccles. How's the papering coming along?'

'Great,' said Springy. 'Only two more pieces and we're finished.'

'Ah,' said Uncle Jock. 'I'll just go and get a saw for this moulding.'

He disappeared, quietly, like a vole. There was a pause.

'Well,' said Mrs Price. 'What do you think?'

Mr Price ruffled Springy's hair with one hand, and Sam's with the other.

'An uncle in the attic,' he said. 'Very good.'